Engelbert the Elephant

WRITTEN BY
TOM PAXTON

ILLUSTRATED BY
STEVEN KELLOGG

MORROW JUNIOR BOOKS
NEW YORK

1 2 3 4 5 6 7 8 9 10
Library of Congress Cataloging-in-Publication Data
Paxton, Tom.
Engelbert the elephant / by Tom Paxton;
illustrated by Steven Kellogg.
p.   cm.
Summary: An elephant's dancing skills
and good manners surprise everyone
at the royal ball, including the queen.
ISBN 0-688-08935-6.   ISBN 0-688-08936-4 (lib. bdg.)
[1. Elephants—Fiction.   2. Dancing—Fiction.   3 Stories in
rhyme.]   I. Kellogg, Steven, ill.   II. Title.
PZ8.3.P2738En   1990
[E]—dc20   89-9376   CIP   AC

To Midge, for everything
T.P.

To my beloved friend Helen
S.K.

By Order of HER MAJESTY

THE QUEEN

AN INVITATION
TO THE
ROYAL BALL
IS HEREBY BESTOWED
UPON
ENGELBERT
THE ELEPHANT

To relieve her royal boredom,
the Queen announced a dance.

Invitations were delivered
And it happened quite by chance,

Through an oversight of someone's~
Whose it was I can't recall~

Engelbert the Elephant
was invited to the ball.

Such excitement in the jungle!
Such a holy hullabaloo!
Such a race to find a costume
And to learn a step or two!

You could feel the jungle shaking
(And I'm sure it's shaking yet)
While Engelbert was learning
How to dance the minuet.

The village lamps were lighted.
The sun was going down,
When shrieks of fear and frantic cries
Were heard across the town.

"An elephant is coming!"
"Call the army! Rouse the guard!"

The troops surrounded Engelbert
Outside the palace yard.
The officers in chorus cried,
"You'll have to leave this place!

There'll be no riffraff at the ball
By order of Her Grace!"

But Engelbert astounded them
By pulling from his vest
The document that proved he was
The royal couple's guest.

So the soldiers formed an escort
And they led him to the ball,
Where the orchestra stopped playing
And a hush went through the hall.

Though the King and Queen were speechless
(And I'm sure they're speechless now),
Engelbert the Elephant
Made a very lovely bow.

"How shocking!" cried a duchess.
"It's a scandal!" humphed an earl.

"That horrid beast will *trample* us!"
Exclaimed a foolish girl.

Then panic seized the courtiers.
The banquet was upset.

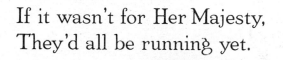

If it wasn't for Her Majesty,
They'd all be running yet.

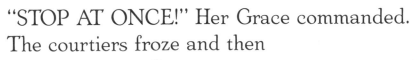

"STOP AT ONCE!" Her Grace commanded.
The courtiers froze and then

The Queen advanced toward Engelbert,
Who bowed to her again.

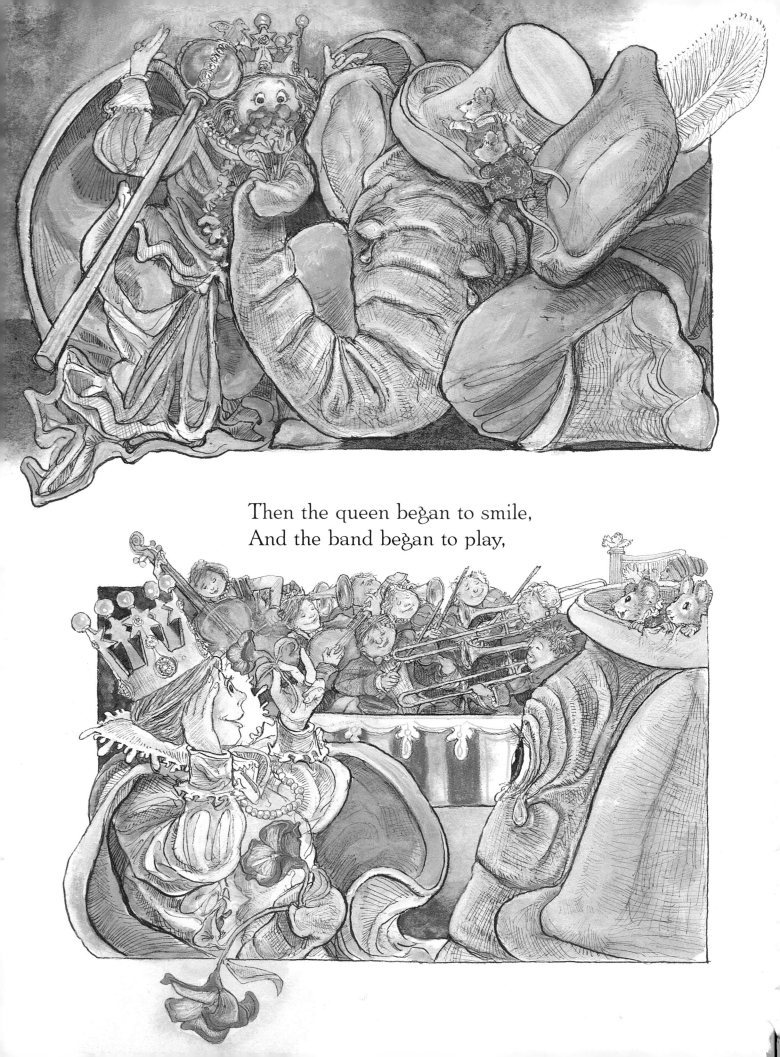

Then the queen began to smile,
And the band began to play,

And Engelbert was dancing
In the very nicest way.

The ladies were delighted
At the way he turned and spun,

And before the night was over,
He had danced with everyone.

When they all sat down to dinner
(Neatly rescued from the floor),
Engelbert just nibbled,
Though he dreamed of eating more.

When the final dance was called for,
Such a sight you've never seen.
For the elephant was chosen
As the partner of the Queen.

Now when the ball was over,
Though the hour was very late,

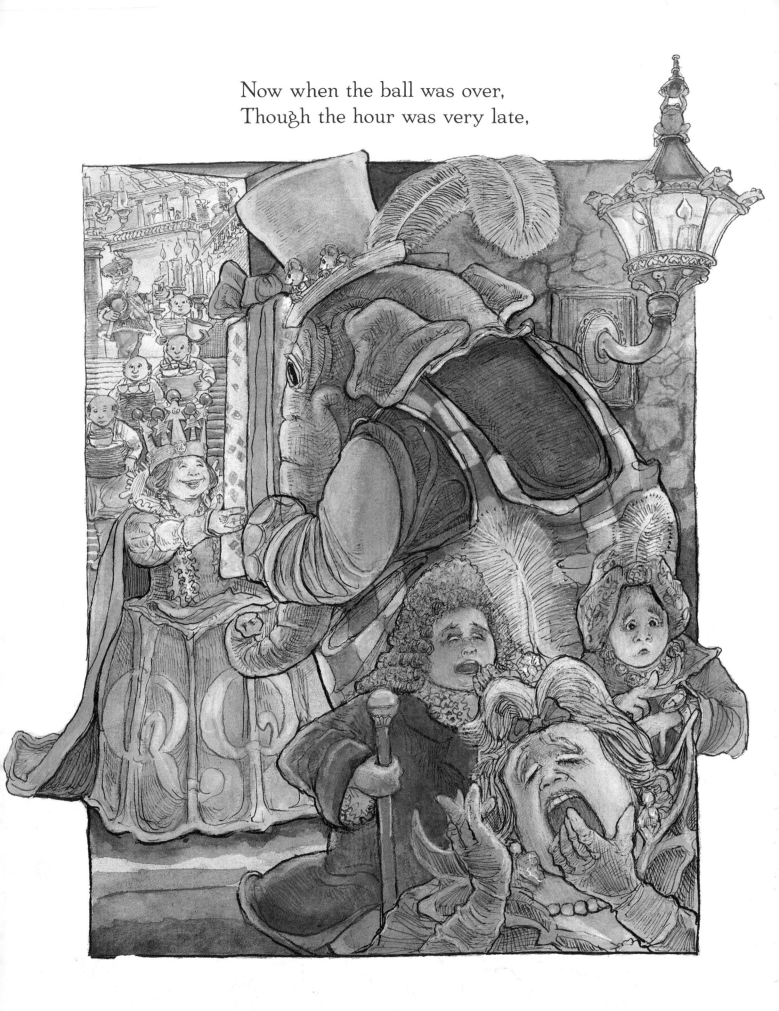

The guests all followed Engelbert
Outside the village gate.

His jungle friends were waiting there;
The band began to play

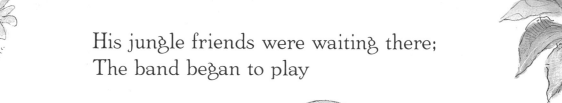

And the frolicking that followed
Is still talked about today.

to my beloved friend
Engelbert,
from your devoted
Queen